D1529728

Bala Kids
An imprint of Shambhala Publications, Inc.
4720 Walnut Street
Boulder, Colorado 80301
www.shambhala.com

9 8 7 6 5 4 3 2 1

First Edition
Printed in China

∞ This edition is printed on acid-free paper that meets the American National Standards
Institute Z39.48 Standard.
♻ Shambhala Publications makes every effort to print on recycled paper.
For more information please visit www.shambhala.com.

Bala Kids is distributed worldwide by Penguin Random House, Inc., and its subsidiaries.

Designed by Kara Plikaitis

Library of Congress Cataloging-in-Publication Data
Names: Becher, Natalie, author.
Title: Krit dreams of dragon fruit: a story of leaving and finding home /
Natalie Becher and Emily France; illustrated by Samantha Woo.
Description: First Edition. | Boulder: Bala Kids, 2020.
Identifiers: LCCN 2018053508 | ISBN 9781611807752 (hardcover: alk. paper)
Subjects: LCSH: Koan—Juvenile literature.
Classification: LCC BQ9289.5 .F73 2019 | DDC 294.3/4432—dc23
LC record available at https://lccn.loc.gov/2018053508

Krit Dreams of Dragon Fruit

A Story of Leaving and Finding Home

Natalie Becher
and Emily France

bala kids

Illustrated by
Samantha Woo

Krit loved his home.

He lived with his dog, Mu, in Thailand, in the city of Chiang Mai.

Mu and Krit went everywhere together.

They raced up tiled temple steps and sped by Naga serpents standing guard.

They ducked under dragon fruit carts in the market, past papaya and longans and red rambutans.

They stood at the foot of the giant Buddha statue,
his gentle smile like a hug for the whole world.

One special night each year, they went to the Ping River for the festival of lights. Krit made a boat of banana leaves. His friends brought sticks of incense and a candle for the mast. The river lit up like the stars had come down for a swim.

Krit made a wish:

Let nothing change.

But at dinner as Krit slipped a handful of rice to Mu, his mother looked up from her plate.

"My sweet son, your aunt and uncle in America have asked us to come help with their shop. So we're moving," she said. "To a city called Chicago."

Krit felt like a tree about to blow down.

His mom gave him a hug and a long, loving look. "You'll feel at home there in no time."

And so things changed.

In Chicago, Mu and Krit visited all sorts of new places.

They climbed to the top of a tall tower.

No Naga serpents. No big Buddha smile.
"No dogs allowed!" a guard shouted.

They searched for fruit in a Logan Square market,
but all they found were apples trapped in jars.

No round, sweet papaya. No red rambutans.
"No dogs allowed!" a vendor shouted.

Krit and Mu trudged by the icy river.

No banana-leaf boats. No floating lights.
No friends.

"This will never be home," Krit said.

That night, Krit felt sad as ever as his mother tucked him in to bed. "Tell me a story about home," he said.

She smiled and sat close, strong and steady as a mountain.

"Buddha pointed to an empty spot in a field and said it would be a good place to build a temple.

Indra, emperor of the gods, plucked a single blade of grass and set it on the ground.

'The temple is already built.'

And Buddha smiled."

Krit wasn't smiling. "How is that a story about home?"

"You'll see," his mother whispered as she planted a kiss on his cheek.

The light went out, but Krit's eyes stayed open wide.

The next day, Krit and Mu slumped in the snow by the same old, cold river. Krit thought of Indra looking at a blade of grass and seeing a temple.

So he looked at the river.

And looked.

And looked.

And this time ...

"A BOAT!"

The mast flickered like a candle. The hull shined like banana leaves. Krit and Mu ran along the slippery riverbank, around a curve, over a bridge, up and down and up again, faster and faster until they bumped right into a girl.

"Hi," Krit said shyly. "I like your boat. I know how to make a boat with leaves, and candles, and incense. It's called a krathong."

"That sounds beautiful!" she said. "And I like your dog."

"That's Mu. I'm Krit. We just moved here."

"I'm Dahlia. Welcome to Chicago! I love this city."

"You *do*?" Krit asked. Mu cocked his head.

"Yes! I'll show you *everything*. And after, will you teach me how to build your boat?"

Krit and Mu followed Dahlia to Logan Square.
She pointed at a pot of hot cider by the apples.

Krit went in to take a closer look. He filled his cup
and took a slow sip, a happy zing on his tongue.
Sweet and bright like dragon fruit.

Krit hid Mu in his jacket and followed Dahlia to the top of the tall tower. She pointed to her apartment, a tiny square of light in the distance.

Krit leaned against the window to take a closer look.

This time, he saw buildings bigger than bodhi trees. The sun a fat juicy slice of papaya. Blinking red lights, electric rambutans in the streets. Scarves flapping in the wind like ribbons of woolly Naga serpents. Winding through it all, the river.

Krit noticed how it curved slow and steady like a smile that was spreading across the city.

A big blue Buddha smile.

Krit had an idea. "Follow me!" he said.

They dashed to Krit's apartment with Mu in tow.

"Mom, Mom!" he yelled. "I saw a boat with a mast like a candle, drank cider sweet as dragon fruit, saw a big Buddha smile, and met …"

He took a long look at Dahlia.

"A friend."

He plucked one blade of grass from the pot just inside the door, bright green like the hills of Chiang Mai.

"I know the secret of the story. I want to go home. But if I take a closer look at things like Indra did, slow and steady, I see I'm already there. I can be home *anywhere*."

And Krit smiled.

A Note from the Authors

Over twenty years ago, we met on the campus of Brown University as undergraduate students. We immediately formed a friendship and spent many evenings studying, sharing thoughts about spirituality and its role in our lives, and having lots of fun too. After graduating, we would make a total of sixteen moves between us, spanning three continents and nine American states. In other words, we learned a thing or two about moving and about change. Our journeys were not easy, and through all of life's ups and downs, we each searched for a sense of solidity in daily storms, a sense of being at home in the middle of change—we both found it in Buddhist practice.

Twenty years later, we reconnected and shared our trials and triumphs, how our Buddhist practices have changed us and help ease that troubling sense that things aren't as they should be. The result is this story.

Krit's tale is a mix of our practices and experiences. Natalie's mother taught her tenets of Buddhism as a child, and Natalie has connected with practices from both Theravada and Mahayana traditions in recent years. Emily finds her spiritual home in Zen. The story Krit's mother tells him is from a koan collection—teachings collected over centuries designed to transmit wisdom and test a student's understanding of Buddhist ideas. They are a bit like word puzzles without set answers; the idea is to experience a koan like Krit does—read it, carry it in your heart, and see if anything in your life starts to look different. But the idea that happiness can't be found by avoiding change or by somehow finding a lasting permanence is a universal Buddhist principal. We are all already home; we just don't always know it.

And wherever you are now, and wherever you are from, we hope this story helps you feel at home every time you read it.

With love,
Natalie and Emily